the
children's
story

Also by James Clavell

KING RAT · TAI-PAN · SHŌGUN · NOBLE HOUSE

the children's story

James Clavell

AN ELEANOR FRIEDE BOOK
in association with Michaela Clavell Crisman

A LAUREL/ELEANOR FRIEDE EDITION

A Laurel/Eleanor Friede Book

Published by
Dell Publishing
a division of
The Bantam Doubleday Dell Publishing Group, Inc.
666 Fifth Avenue
New York, New York 10103

ISBN: 0-440-31227-2

Reprinted by arrangement with Delacorte Press/Eleanor Friede

Printed in the United States of America

October 1982

10 9 8 7 6 5 4 3 2

OPM

For all children
... everywhere

the teacher was afraid.

And the children were afraid. All except Johnny. He watched the classroom door with hate. He felt the hatred deep within his stomach. It gave him strength.

It was two minutes to nine.

The teacher glanced numbly from the door and stared at the flag which stood in a corner of the room. But she couldn't see the flag today. She was blinded by her terror, not only for herself but mostly for them, her children. She had never had children of her own. She had never married.

In the mists of her mind she saw the rows upon rows of children she had taught through her years. Their faces were legion. But she could distinguish no one particular face. Only the same face which varied but slightly. Always the same age or thereabouts. Seven. Perhaps a boy, perhaps a girl. And the face always open and ready for the knowledge that she was to give. The same face staring at her, open, waiting and full of trust.

The children rustled, watching her, wondering what possessed her. They saw not the gray hair and the old eyes and the lined face and the well-worn clothes. They saw only their teacher and the twisting of her hands. Johnny looked away from the door and watched with the other children. He did not understand anything except that the teacher was afraid, and because she was afraid she was making them all worse and he wanted to shout that there was no need to fear. "Just because *they've* conquered us there's no need for panic-fear," Dad had said. "Don't be afraid, Johnny. If you fear too much, you'll be dead even though you're alive."

The sound of footsteps approached and then stopped. The door opened.

The children gasped. They had expected an ogre or giant or beast or witch or monster—like the outer-space monsters you think about when the lights are out and Momma and Daddy have kissed you good night and you're frightened and you put your head under the cover and all at once you're awake and it's time for school. But instead of a monster, a beautiful young girl stood in the doorway. Her clothes were neat and clean, all olive green—even her shoes. But most important, she wore a lovely smile, and when she spoke, she spoke without the trace of an accent. The children found this very strange, for *they* were foreigners from a strange country far across the sea. They had all been told about *them*.

"Good morning, children, I'm your new teacher," the New Teacher said. Then she closed the door softly and walked to the teacher's desk, and the children in the front row felt and smelled the perfume of her—clean and fresh and young—and as she passed Sandra who sat at the end of the first row she said, "Good morning, Sandra," and Sandra flushed deeply and wondered, aghast, with all the other children, *How did she know my name?* and her heart raced in her chest and made it feel tight and very heavy.

The teacher got up shakily. "I, er, I—good morning." Her words were faltering. She, too, was trying to get over the shock. And nausea.

"Hello, Miss Worden," the New Teacher said. "I'm taking over your class now. You are to go to the principal's office."

"Why? What's going to happen to me? What's going to happen to my children?" The words gushed from Miss Worden, and a lank piece of hair fell into her eyes. The children were agonized by the cut to her voice, and one or two of them felt on the edge of tears.

"He just wants to talk to you, Miss Worden," the New Teacher said gently. "You really must take better care of yourself. You shouldn't be so upset."

Miss Worden saw the New Teacher's smile but she wasn't touched by its compassion. She tried to stop her knees from shaking. "Good-bye, children," she said. The children made no reply. They were too terrified by the sound of her voice and the tears that wet her face. And because she was crying, some of the children cried, and Sandra fled to her.

The New Teacher shut the door behind Miss Worden and turned back into the room, cradling Sandra in her arms. "Children, children, there's no need to cry!" she said. "I know. I'll sing you a song! Listen!"

And she sat down on the floor as gracefully as an angel, Sandra in her arms, and she began to sing and the children stopped crying because Miss Worden never, never sang to them and certainly never sat on the floor, which is the best place to sit, as everyone in the class knew. They listened spellbound to the happy lilt of the New Teacher's voice and to the strange words of a strange tongue which soared and dipped like the sea of grass that was the birthplace of the song. It was a child's song and it soothed them, and after she had sung the first chorus the New Teacher told them the story of the song.

It was about two children who had lost their way and were all alone in the great grass prairies and were afraid, but they met a fine man riding a fine horse and the man told them that there was never a need to be afraid, for all they had to do was to watch the stars and the stars would tell them where their home was.

"For once you know the right direction, then there's never a need to be afraid. Fear is something that comes from inside, from inside your tummies," the New Teacher said radiantly, "and good strong children like you have to put food in your tummies. Not fear."

The children thought about this and it seemed very sensible. The New Teacher sang the song again, and soon all the children were happy and calm once more. Except Johnny. He hated her even though he knew she was right about fear.

"Now," said the New Teacher, "what shall we do? I know, we'll play a game. I'll try and guess your names!"

The children, wide-eyed, shifted in their seats. Miss Worden never did this, and often she called a child by another's name. *The New Teacher'll never know all our names! Never!* they thought. So they waited excitedly while the New Teacher turned her attention to Sandra. Oh, yes, somehow she already knew Sandra's name, but how could she possibly know everyone's? They waited, glad that they were going to catch out the New Teacher.

But they were not to catch her out. The New Teacher remembered every name!

Johnny put up his hand. "How'd you know our names? I mean, well, we haven't had a roll call or anything, so how'd you know our names?"

"That's easy, Johnny," the New Teacher said. "You all sit in the same places every day. Each desk has one pupil. So I learned your names from a list. I had to work for three whole days to remember your names. A teacher must work very hard to be a good teacher, and so I worked for three days so that I could know each of you the first day. That's very important, don't you think, for a teacher to work hard?"

Johnny frowned and half-nodded and sat down and wondered why he hadn't figured that out for himself before asking, astonished that she had worked three days just to know everyone the first day. But still he hated her.

"Johnny. Would you tell me something, please? How do you start school? I mean what do you do to begin with?"

Johnny stood reluctantly. "We first pledge allegiance and then we sing the song—"

"Yes, but that's all after roll call," Sandra said. "You forgot roll call."

"Yes. You forgot roll call, Johnny," Mary said.

"First we have roll call," Johnny said. Then he sat down.

The New Teacher smiled. "All right. But we really don't need roll call. I know all your names and I know everyone's here. It's very lazy for a teacher not to know who's here and who isn't, don't you think? After all, a teacher should *know*. So we don't need roll call while I'm your teacher. So we should pledge, isn't that next?"

Obediently all the children got up and put their hands on their hearts and the New Teacher did the same, and they began in unison, "I pledge allegiance to the flag of—"

"Just a moment," the New Teacher said. "What does *pledge* mean?"

The children stood openmouthed; Miss Worden had never interrupted them before. They stood and stared at the New Teacher. Wordless. And silent.

"What does *allegiance* mean?" the New Teacher asked, her hand over her heart.

The children stood in silence. Then Mary put up her hand. "Well, *pledge* is, ah, well, something like—sort of when you want to do something very good. You sort of pledge you're going to do something like not suck your thumb 'cause that makes your teeth bend and you'll have to wear a brace and go to the dentist, which hurts."

"That's very good, Mary. Very, very good. To pledge means to promise. And *allegiance*?"

Mary shrugged helplessly and looked at her best friend, Hilda, who looked back at her and then at the teacher and shrugged helplessly too.

The New Teacher waited, and the silence hung in the room, hurting. Then she said, "I think it's quite wrong for you to have to say something with long words in it if you don't understand what you're saying."

So the children sat down and waited expectantly.

"What did your other teacher tell you that it meant?"

After a long silence Danny put up his hand. "She never said nothing, miss."

"One of my teachers at the other school I went to before this one," Joan said in a rush, "well, she sort of said what it all meant, at least she said something about it just before recess one day and then the bell went and afterwards we had spellin'."

Danny said, "Miss Worden—well, she never told us. We just hadta learn it and then say it, that's all. Our real teacher didn't say anything at all."

All the children nodded. Then they waited again.

"Your teacher never explained to you?" All the children shook their heads.

"I don't think that was very good. Not to explain. You can always ask me anything. That's what a real teacher should do." Then the New Teacher said, "But didn't you ask your daddies and mommies?"

"Not about 'I pledge.' We just hadta learn it," Mary said. "Once I could say it, Daddy gave me a nickel for saying it good."

"That's right," Danny said. "So long as you could say it all, it was very good. But I never got no nickel."

"Did you ask each other what it meant?"

"I askt Danny once and he didn't know and none of us knowed really. It's grown-up talk, and grown-ups talk that sort of words. We just havta learn it."

"The other schools I went to," Hilda said, "they never said anything about it. They just wanted us to learn it. They didn't ask us what it meant. We just hadta say it every day before we started school."

"It took me weeks and weeks and weeks to say it right," Mary said.

So the New Teacher explained what *allegiance* meant. "...so you are promising or pledging support to the flag and saying that it is much more important than *you* are. How can a flag be more important than a real live person?"

Johnny broke the silence. "But the next thing is—well, where it says 'and to the republic for which it stands.' That means it's like a, like a..." He searched for the word and could not find it. "Like a well, sort of sign, isn't it?"

"Yes. The real word is a *symbol*." The New Teacher frowned. "But we don't need a sign to remind us that we love our country, do we? You're all good boys and girls. Do you need a sign to remind you?"

"What's *remind* mean?" Mary asked.

"It means to make you remember. To make you remember that you're all good boys and girls."

The children thought about this and shook their heads.

Johnny put up his hand. "It's our flag," he said fiercely. "We always pledge."

"Yes," the New Teacher said. "It *is* a very pretty one." She looked at it a moment and then said, "I wish I could have a piece of it. If it's so important, I think we should all have a piece of it. Don't you?"

"I've a little one at home," Mary said. "I could bring it tomorrow."

"Thank you, Mary dear, but I just wanted a little piece of this one because it's our own special classroom one."

Then Danny said, "If we had some scissors we could cut a little piece off."

"I've some scissors at home," Mary said.

"There's some in Miss Worden's desk," Brian said.

The New Teacher found the scissors and then they had to decide who would be allowed to cut a little piece off, and the New Teacher said that because today was Mary's birthday (*How did you know that?* Mary asked herself, awed) Mary should be allowed to cut the piece off. And then they decided it would be very nice if they all had a piece. The flag is special, they thought, so if you have a piece, that's better than having just to look at it, 'cause you can keep it in your pocket.

So the flag was cut up by the children and they were very proud that they each had a piece. But now the flagpole was barc and strange.

And useless.

The children pondered what to do with it, and the idea that pleased them most was to push it out of the window. They watched excitedly as the New Teacher opened the window and allowed them to throw it into the playground. They shrieked with excitement as they saw it bounce on the ground and lie there. They began to love this strange New Teacher.

When they were all back in their seats the New Teacher said, "Well, before we start our lessons, perhaps there are some questions you want me to answer. Ask me anything you like. That's only fair, isn't it, if I ask you questions?"

Mary said, after a silence, "We never get to ask our real teacher *any* questions."

"You can always ask me anything. That's the fair way. The new way. Try me."

"What's your name?" Danny asked.

She told them her name, and it sounded pretty.

Mary put up her hand. "Why do you wear those clothes? Well, it's like a sort of uniform nurses wear."

"We think that teachers should be dressed the same. Then you always know a teacher. It's nice and light and easy to iron. Do you like the color?"

"Oh, yes," Mary said. "You've got green eyes too."

"If you like, children, as a very special surprise, you can all have this sort of uniform. Then you won't have to worry about what you have to wear to school every day. And you'll all be the same."

The children twisted excitedly in their seats. Mary said, "But it'll cost a lot, and my momma won't want to spend the money 'cause we have to buy food and food is expen— Well, it sort of costs a lot of money."

"They will be given to you. As a present. There's no need to worry about money."

Johnny said, "I don't want to be dressed like that."

"You don't have to accept a present, Johnny. Just because the other children want to wear new clothes, you don't have to," the New Teacher said.

Johnny slunk back in his chair. *I'm never going to wear their clothes,* he said to himself. *I don't care if I'm going to look different from Danny and Tom and Fred.*

Then Mary asked, "Why was our teacher crying?"

"I suppose she was just tired and needed a rest. She's going to have a long rest." She smiled at them. "We think teachers should be young. I'm nineteen."

"Is the war over now?" Danny asked.

"Yes, Danny, isn't that wonderful! Now all your daddies will be home soon."

"Did we win or did we lose?" Mary asked.

"We—that's you and I and all of us— *we* won."

"Oh!"

The children sat back happily.

Then Johnny's hatred burst. "Where's my dad? What've you done to my dad? Where's my dad?"

The New Teacher got up from her seat and walked the length of the room and the children's eyes followed her, and Johnny stood, knees of jelly. She sat down on his seat and put her hands on his shoulders, and his shoulders were shaking like his knees.

"He's going to a school. Some grown-ups have to go to school as well as children."

"But they took him away and he didn't want to go." Johnny felt the tears close and he fought them back.

The New Teacher touched him gently, and he smelled the youth and cleanness of her, and it was not the smell of home which was sour and just a little dirty. "He's no different from all of you. *You* sometimes don't want to go to school. With grown-ups it's the same—just the same as children. Would you like to visit him? He has a holiday in a few days."

"Momma said that Dad's gone away forever!" Johnny stared at her incredulously. "He has a holiday?"

The New Teacher laughed. "She's wrong, Johnny. After all, everyone who goes to school has holidays. That's fair, isn't it?"

The children shifted and rustled and watched. And Johnny said, "I can see him?"

"Of course. Your daddy just has to go back to school a little. He had some strange thoughts, and he wanted other grown-ups to believe them. It's not right to want others to believe wrong thoughts, is it?"

"Well, no, I suppose not. But my dad never thought nothing bad."

"Of course, Johnny. I said *wrong* thoughts—not *bad* thoughts. There's nothing wrong with that. But it's right to show grown-ups right thoughts when they're wrong, isn't it?"

"Well, yes," Johnny said. "But what wrong thoughts did he have?"

"Just some grown-up thoughts that are old-fashioned. We're going to learn all about them in class. Then we can share knowledge, and I can learn from you as you will learn from me. Shall we?"

"All right." Johnny stared at her, perplexed. "My dad couldn't have wrong thoughts. He just couldn't....

Could he?"

"Well, perhaps sometime when you wanted to talk about something very important to your dad, perhaps he said, 'Not now, Johnny, I'm busy,' or, 'We'll talk about that tomorrow.' That's a bad thought —not to give you time when it's important. Isn't it?"

"Sure. But that's what all grown-ups do."

"My momma says that all the time," Mary said.

And the other children nodded, and they wondered if all their parents should go back to school and unlearn bad thoughts.

"Sit down, Johnny, and we'll start learning good things and not worry about grown-up bad thoughts. Oh, yes," she said when she sat down at her seat again, brimming with happiness. "I have a lovely surprise for you. You're all going to stay overnight with us. We have a lovely room and beds and lots of food, and we'll all tell stories and have such a lovely time."

"Oh, good," the children said.

"Can I stay up till eight o'clock?" Mary asked breathlessly.

"Well, as it's our first new day, we'll all stay up to eight-thirty. But only if you promise to go right to sleep afterward."

The children all promised. They were very happy. Jenny said, "But first we got to say our prayers. Before we go to sleep."

The New Teacher smiled at her. "Of course. Perhaps we should say a prayer now. In some schools that's a custom too." She thought a moment, and the faces watched her. Then she said, "Let's pray. But let's pray for something very good. What should we pray for?"

"Bless Momma and Daddy," Danny said immediately.

"That's a good idea, Danny. I have one. Let's pray for candy. That's a good idea, isn't it?"

They all nodded happily.

So, following their New Teacher, they all closed their eyes and steepled their hands together, and they prayed with her for candy.

The New Teacher opened her eyes and looked around disappointedly. "But where's our candy? God is all-seeing and is everywhere, and if we pray, He answers our prayers. Isn't that true?"

"I prayed for a puppy of my own lots of times, but I never got one," Danny said.

"Maybe we didn't pray hard enough. Perhaps we should kneel down like it's done in church."

So the New Teacher knelt and all the children knelt and they prayed very, very hard. But there was still no candy.

Because the New Teacher was disappointed, the children were very disappointed. Then she said, "Perhaps we're using the wrong name." She thought a moment and then said, "Instead of saying 'God,' let's say 'Our Leader.' Let's pray to Our Leader for candy. Let's pray very hard and don't open your eyes till I say."

So the children shut their eyes tightly and prayed very hard, and as they prayed, the New Teacher took out some candy from her pocket and quietly put a piece on each child's desk. She did not notice Johnny—alone of all the children—

watching her through his half-closed eyes.

She went softly back to her desk and the prayer ended, and the children opened their eyes and they stared at the candy and they were overjoyed.

"I'm going to pray to Our Leader every time," Mary said excitedly.

"Me too," Hilda said. "Could we eat Our Leader's candy now, teacher?"

"Oh, let's, please, please, please."

"So Our Leader answered your prayers, didn't he?"

"I saw you put the candy on our desks!" Johnny burst out. "*I saw you....*

I didn't close my eyes, and I saw you. You had 'em in your pocket. We didn't get them with praying. *You* put them there."

All the children, appalled, stared at him and then at their New Teacher. She stood at the front of the class and looked back at Johnny and then at all of them.

"Yes, Johnny, you're quite right. You're a very, very wise boy. Children, *I* put the candy on your desks. So you know that it doesn't matter whom you ask, whom you shut your eyes and 'pray' to—to God or anyone, even Our Leader—no one will give you anything. Only another human being." She looked at Danny. "God didn't give you the puppy you wanted. But if you work hard, I will. Only I or someone like me can *give* you things. Praying to God or anything or anyone for something is a waste of time."

"Then we don't say prayers? We're not supposed to say prayers?"

The puzzled children watched her.

"You can if you want to, children. If your daddies and mommies want you to. But we know, you and I, that it means nothing. That's our secret."

"My dad says it's wrong to have secrets from him."

"But he has secrets that he shares with your mommy and not with you, doesn't he?"

All the children nodded.

"Then it's not wrong for us to have a few secrets from them. Is it?"

"I like having secrets. Hilda and me have lots of secrets," Mary said.

The New Teacher said, "We're going to have lots of wonderful secrets together. You can eat your candy if you want to. And because Johnny was especially clever, I think we should make him monitor for the whole week, don't you?"

They all nodded happily and popped the candy into their mouths and chewed gloriously. Johnny was very proud as he chewed his candy; he decided that he liked his teacher very much. Because she told the truth. Because she was right about fear. Because she was right about God. He'd prayed many times for many things and never got them, and even the one time he did get the skates, he knew his dad had heard him and had put them under his bed for his birthday and pretended he hadn't heard him. *I always wondered why He didn't listen, and all the time He wasn't there,* he thought.

Johnny sat back contentedly, resolved to work hard and listen and not to have wrong thoughts like Dad.

The teacher waited for them to finish their candy. This was what she had been trained for, and she knew that she would teach her children well and that they would grow up to be good citizens. She looked out of the window, at the sun over the land. It was a good land, and vast. A land to breathe in. But she was warmed not by the sun but by the thought that throughout the school and throughout the land all children, all men and all women were being taught with the same faith, with variations of the same procedures. Each according to his age group. Each according to his need.

She glanced at her watch....

It was 9:23.

That fall she was almost six
and she came home from first
school — almost first day — and
said in a proud rush: "Daddy
Daddy, listen: "I plege 'illequence
to the flag..."

Her tiny hand was over her
heart and when she had finished
the blur of words she peered up at
me. "There," she said breathlessly
and held out her hand.

"There what, my darling?"

"You owe me a dime!"

"Oh? What for?"

"The plege illequence. Didn't I

say it right? Oh, I'm sure I did. Didn't I?"

"Oh. Oh yes, yes, I think you did." At that time I was not a citizen. "But why a dime?"

"The teacher said everyone has to learn it and say it and then your dad or mum gives you a dime. That's what the teacher said."

I paid her.

"Thank you," she said, very satisfied. "How about another dime if I say it again?"

"One dime at a time. By the way, what's pledge mean?"

"Huh?"

"Pledge? Allegiance?"

She was perplexed. "Plege' ill-egience is plege'illegience!"

"Didn't your teacher explain what you were learning? Any of those long words?"

Her frown deepened. "We've to learn it and say it and then we get a dime. That's what our teacher said." Then she added happily, "I know I said it right. I was better than Johnny..."

During that day I asked all kinds of people of every age, "You know the 'I pledge allegiance...'"

but before I could finish, at once they would all parrot it, the words almost always equally slurred. In every case I discovered that not one teacher, ever — or anyone — had ever explained the words to any one of them. Everyone just had to learn it to say it.

The Children's Story came into being that day. It was then that I realised how completely vulnerable my child's mind was → any mind for that matter → under controlled circumstances.

Normally I write and rewrite and re-rewrite, but this story came quickly —— almost by itself. Barely three words were changed. It pleases me greatly because it keeps asking me questions....

Questions like What's the use of "I pledge allegiance" without understanding? Like Why is it so easy to divert thoughts and implant others? Like What is freedom and why is it so hard to explain?

<u>The Children's Story</u> keeps

asking me all sorts of questions
I cannot answer.

Perhaps you can ——— then
your child will....

Lookout Mountain,
California